For my grandmother, Sophia Morton – F.H.

LADYBIRD BOOKS, INC.
Auburn, Maine 04210 U.S.A.
© LADYBIRD BOOKS LTD 1990
Loughborough, Leicestershire, England

All rights reserved. No part of this publication may be reproduced, stored in a retrieval system, or transmitted in any form or by any means, electronic, mechanical, photocopying, recording or otherwise, without the prior consent of the copyright owner.

Printed in England

Joshua at Jericho

Retold by Fern Howard
Illustrated by Tom Sperling

Ladybird Books

Moses had led the people of Israel for many years toward a land where God had promised they could live in peace. But when Moses died, the Israelites had not yet entered the promised land. So God called Joshua to guide his people to their new home.

God said to Joshua, "Be strong and brave, and obey my laws, and you will be successful in everything you do. Remember, the Lord is with you wherever you go."

Some of the Israelites were living on one side of the Jordan River. But Moses had told them they could not settle there for good until they helped win the land on the other side of the river.

To get to the other side of the river, the Israelites had to cross it on foot. The Jordan was deep and wide and overflowing its banks.

But when the Israelites wanted to go across, the Lord caused the water to stop flowing and pile up far upstream. The people easily crossed the dry riverbed. As soon as the last person was on the other side, the water came rushing down again.

But God told Joshua what to do. The Israelites made a great procession. First came soldiers, then seven priests with trumpets of ram's horn, then more priests to carry the Ark with the stone tablets of the Ten Commandments, and more soldiers.

"Everyone must be silent except for the trumpets," Joshua commanded. "Do not say a word until I tell you to shout!" And he began to lead the troops in a parade around the city walls.

Joshua and the Israelites marched once around the city that day. No one said a word, but the priests blew their horns without stopping.

For six days, Joshua led the troops once around Jericho in exactly the same way, just as the sun began to rise. Afterward, they returned to their camp and waited for the next day.

On the seventh day, they started out as usual. But this time, the Israelites circled Jericho not once, but seven times. The seventh time, as the priests blew their trumpets long and hard, Joshua commanded, "Shout! The Lord has given us the city."

The people shouted as loud as they could, and the priests blew their horns. At the noise of the trumpets and the voices, the walls of Jericho crumbled before the Israelites' eyes!